THERE IS
NO BIG BAD WOLF
IN THIS STORY

Wake Up Wolf

You are LATE

You are very LATE

Last Chance!

For Joe and Nell - L.C.

For Rae - D.A.

BLOOMSBURY CHILDREN'S BOOKS
Bloomsbury Publishing Plc
50 Bedford Square, London, WC1B 3DP, UK
29 Earlsfort Terrace, Dublin 2, Ireland

First published in Great Britain in 2021
by Bloomsbury Publishing Plc

Printed and bound in China by Leo Paper Products, Heshan, Guangdong

A catalogue record for this book is available from the British Library

BLOOMSBURY, BLOOMSBURY CHILDREN'S BOOKS and the Diana logo are trademarks of Bloomsbury Publishing Plc

To find out more about our authors and books visit www.bloomsbury.com and sign up for our newsletters

ISBN 978 1 5266 0817 8 (HB)

ISBN 978 1 5266 0816 1 (PB)

ISBN 978 1 5266 0819 2 (eBook)

2 4 6 8 10 9 7 5 3 1

THERE IS NO BIG BAD WOLF IN THIS STORY

LOU CARTER

DEBORAH ALLWRIGHT

BLOOMSBURY

LONDON OXFORD NEW YORK NEW DELHI SYDNEY

This was supposed to be a story about a Big Bad Wolf

YIKES!

. . . who tricked Little Red

NAUGHTY!

then chased little piggies . . .

OINK!

... and blew down
their houses -

HUMPH!

but fell

down

the

chimney

(WHICH SERVED HIM
JOLLY WELL RIGHT!)

The end.

However, I can't tell you that story because this Big Bad Wolf is late! AGAIN!

"Yes, yes, yes, I KNOW I'm late! You have NO idea how hard it is being me!"

The Three Little Pigs are seriously grumpy.

"All your huffing and puffing should have been over and done by now!"

says the First Little Pig.

"Where have you BEEN?"

says the Second Little Pig.

"We can't sit around here all day waiting for you!"

says the Third Little Pig.

But Wolf can't stop . . .

GRANDMA'S HOUSE

LITTLE PIGS

He must get to
Grandma's house

before Little Red Riding
Hood arrives.

"Get a move on, Mr Wolf! You're supposed to be in OUR story!" says Grandma.

Poor Wolf. He is absolutely **frazzled.**

It's completely IMPOSSIBLE and you are ALWAYS cross with me and I WON'T put up with it anymore. From now on, there will be NO Big Bad Wolf in ANY of your stories!"

HUMPH!

They can totally manage without him!

Can't they?

Can't they?

Everyone tries their best . . .

But Big Bad Wolfing...

...is MUCH harder than it looks!

Fortunately, **Dragon** has come to help!

He will be **excellent** at huffing and puffing . . .

Or maybe not!

Huffing and puffing is **not** the best job for a dragon.

What a disaster!

"We really need a BIG, BAD WOLF in this story!"

says Little Red Riding Hood.

"But where IS he?"

says the Gingerbread Man.

Ah-ha! Here he is . . .

"Please, PLEASE help us, Mr Wolf!
All our stories are burning down!"
says Grandma.

"And no one can huff and puff like YOU!"
says the Second Little Pig.

But Wolf doesn't **want** to help . . .

Does he?

Does he?

He DOES!

No one can huff and puff like a
Big, Bad WOLF!

Wolf has saved the day!

"We're SUPER sorry we were cross with you," says the First Little Pig.

"And we promise to **help** you from now on," says the Second Little Pig.

"We totally can't manage
without you!"

. . . so they gave him
a helping hand –

GO TEAM!

and he was never late again!

The end.